GRIMLOCK PRISON

Laura Shenton

GRIMLOCK PRISON

Laura Shenton

Iridescent Toad Publishing

Iridescent Toad Publishing.

Cover by Blackstone Book Cover Design.

First edition. ISBN: 978-1-913779-23-8

Chapter One

The frigid night air blasted through the narrow openings in the bus window's iron bars, whipping Kerri's long dark hair against her cheeks and causing her skin to tingle with discomfort. She was perched on a hard, unforgiving seat, cuffed at the ankles and wrists, with a heavy chain wrapped around her hips to keep everything in place. The long journey had been filled with endless bumps and jolts, making every movement painful and frustrating. Now though, as the prison bus wheezed to a stop, she knew that the real challenge was just beginning.

The wearied atmosphere of the bus resonated with tired voices, each a note in a symphony of exhaustion.

"I could use a drink right about now," said one woman, slouched in her seat. "This whole ordeal's driving me to the brink."

"I miss my bed," another said with a heavy sigh, capturing the sentiment of many.

Kerri's keen gaze swept across the motley crew of women on the bus; each one of them bore the distinctive and unmistakable essence of their paranormal identity. It was a strange and eclectic mix of witches, shifters and fae, their unique auras blending together awkwardly in the confined space.

Agitation hung in the air like an oppressive fog, making the cramped bus feel even smaller. Some of the women were loud, chattering endlessly and attempting to dominate the space. Others sat there quietly, resigned to the inevitable, silent shadows of their former selves.

The collective sense of anticipation heightened when the bus door creaked and hissed, piercing the uneasy atmosphere and causing everyone to shudder. The floodlights from outside cast an intense brightness into the vehicle, revealing the figure of a stern-faced prison guard standing to attention. His sharp features and rigid posture sent a clear message to all those on board; there would be no room for defiance or disobedience.

"Alright, you freaks, welcome to your new

home!" barked the guard, his voice echoing through the bus. "Single-file line, ro talking, no funny business."

Kerri struggled to stand up, feeling the oppressive weight of her chains dragging her down like anchors. The heavy steel rubbed uncomfortably against her wrists and ankles, a constant reminder of her confinement. She looked around at the other inmates, their faces etched with fear, fury, or indifference. Some mirrored her trepidation, whilst others wore smirks or stoic expressions, hiding their true emotions.

Still unused to her chains, Kerri stumbled forward, the metal biting into her skin with each step. It was an effort to maintain her balance. She could feel her anger flaring, but she knew better than to let it show. She had never been to prison before and didn't want to draw attention to herself.

Just keep moving, she thought. *One step at a time.*

As the prisoners stepped off the bus, another guard began calling out names. Bewildered, Kerri looked up at the looming building before her. The concrete seemed to mock her, a visual reminder of the abrupt shift her life had taken. As a first-time prisoner, uncertainty gripped her. An outsider now turned inmate, the gravity of her situation settled upon her like a heavy cloak. Her eyes scanned the foreboding structure, searching for any sign of solace or familiarity amidst the gloom. However, the high walls offered nothing but an intimidating silence.

"Kerri Hawthorne!"

At the shock of hearing her name, Kerri hesitated, her heart thudding urgently in her chest. It all felt so surreal, as though she was trapped in some twisted nightmare.

"Present," she mumbled, raising her chained hands slightly.

The guard nodded curtly and gestured for her to join a smaller group who were due to be led into the prison building.

"Move it!" another guard snapped from behind her, his aggressive baritone causing her to shudder as he gave her a shove.

Kerri swallowed hard, her throat dry from fear.

She looked back at the bus, desperately wishing for a glimpse of her sister, Mehgan. They had been separated, and she couldn't shake the worry that gnawed at her insides.

"Move!" the guard behind her yelled again, pushing her more forcefully this time. "I won't tell you again."

Kerri moved with a reluctant shuffle towards the group she had been assigned to. The cold steel restraints hindered her every step, each clink of metal resonating like a melancholic echo of lost freedom. She cast fleeting glances at the diverse assembly around her, a silent acknowledgment shared in the language of captivity.

I've got to find Mehgan.

Two burly prison guards, stern sentinels of authority, guided the group with unwavering watchfulness. Kerri's movements were a choreography of submission, a dance dictated by the heavy chains that bound her. The journey towards the prison entrance was a slow procession, the metallic echo of shackles underscoring the weight of her newfound reality.

Her eyes adjusting to the darkness as she set foot

inside the prison, Kerri cautiously looked around, a stark feeling of disappointment and dread clouding her mind. The place seemed to defy the passage of time, as if the concrete walls and high ceiling held memories centuries old of lives lived in captivity. Even the stone floor beneath her felt worn, bearing the echoes of countless footsteps that had trodden the same path of uncertainty. With the air thick and heavy, carrying a damp, musty stench, the prison could have easily passed for a dungeon.

"Line up against the wall!" barked a portly guard with an unusually thin nose, a sneer twisting his face as he watched the inmates shuffle into position. "You'll be split into smaller groups for processing."

"Processing? We're not cattle!" muttered an older prisoner under her breath, her eyes blazing with defiance.

Fear gnawing at her insides, Kerri was both shocked and impressed by the woman's boldness.

"Quiet!" the guard snapped, shooting the woman a glare that promised retribution. "You will follow orders. Is that clear?"

A chorus of begrudging murmurs rippled through the line of prisoners.

"Good. Move when your name is called."

One by one, the inmates were herded towards doors marked with different symbols – a flame, a pair of wings, a crescent moon. Each door led to a room where they would have to undergo various tests and procedures.

"Kerri Hawthorne," called out the guard, his voice devoid of any emotion.

Kerri stepped forward, trying to control the panic bubbling within her chest.

"Through the door with the flame," said the guard, pointing to the leftmost door.

Grimlock Prison

Chapter Two

Hours of processing had passed. Kerri's patience was wearing thin. The cold, damp floor beneath her feet did little to comfort her as she awaited further instructions.

As she stood in the cramped waiting room, her mind wandered back to the event that had landed her here. She and Mehgan had set fire to the city library. They were only witches in play, trying out a new spell they'd discovered in an ancient tome. The spell was meant to be harmless, but in their unfamiliarity with it, everything had escalated beyond their control.

Kerri thought back to the panic that had surged through her veins as she had stood in shock, watching as the flames licked at the bookshelves, consuming the priceless volumes. In a matter of minutes, the once-grand library had been reduced to ashes and smouldering rubble. The guilt of having destroyed such a valuable source of knowledge weighed heavily on her conscience.

Avoiding eye contact with everyone present, Kerri glanced around the busy processing room, searching for any sign of her sister. Although she knew Mehgan would be somewhere in the prison, awaiting her own cell assignment, it terrified her to think that they could have been placed in separate wings.

Where the hell is she?

"Take this," a disinterested guard said, his gruff voice almost a grunt as he shoved a bundle of prison uniform and minimal toiletries into Kerri's arms.

The coarse fabric of the spare bright orange prison uniform lightly scratched her skin as she clutched it tightly, her knuckles whitening. Still with limited mobility due to her shackles, she didn't want to drop anything.

"Can you believe this shit?" a woman next to her said with a sneer as she gestured towards their meagre belongings.

The woman's voice dripped with disdain, and her eyes were like daggers, daring anyone to challenge her.

Trying to appear unfazed by the woman's aggression, Kerri replied with a compliant nod of her head, making a conscious effort not to engage further unless she absolutely had to.

She scanned the faces of the other inmates, desperately trying to catch a glimpse of Mehgan. The sour stench of sweat and fear hung heavy in the cramped room as the reality of the situation settled like a thick fog around her.

Amidst the distant echoes of clinking chains and hushed murmurs, Kerri's heightened senses caught the sound of new prisoners entering the processing room.

Please let Mehgan be here.

Kerri's heart quickened, and with a hopeful urgency, she turned around to scan the influx of unfamiliar faces.

Bingo!

Her eyes lit up as she spotted Mehgan, the

frantic need to shout her sister's name bubbling within her.

"Mehg..."

"No talking during processing!" a guard intercepted, his fetid breath just inches away from Kerri's face.

Kerri's mouth snapped shut, frustration etched on her features. She wanted so badly to shout and scream, to shove the bastard guard away and out of her space, but as a new prisoner, she thought better of it.

Unable to get Mehgan's attention from the other side of the busy processing area, all Kerri could do was watch. Seeing her younger sister in chains caused her to clench her fists, anger coursing through her veins. It wasn't fair; they had just been having some fun, experimenting with their magic, but their powers had betrayed them, spiralling out of control and setting the city library aflame. Now here they were, locked up with the worst of the worst.

It made Kerri feel awful to think that Mehgan might have to do her sentence in another part of the prison. Although they were both strong, and each unique in their own way, as the older sister, Kerri couldn't help but feel responsible for what had happened.

20

Chapter Three

The metallic clanking of her heavy chains reverberated through the dimly lit corridor as Kerri was marched down to her cell. Her long dark hair hung limply around her sharp features, and her eyes were red-rimmed from exhaustion. Despite this, she held her head high, her jaw clenched with a fierce determination that belied her weariness.

"Fuck this shit," grumbled an inmate behind her, her voice echoing off the stone walls. "They haven't even bothered to feed us."

"Tell me about it," another chimed in. "I'm bloody starving!"

Kerri's stomach growled in agreement, but she didn't have the energy to join the women in their complaints. All she could think about was finding Mehgan, and making sure she was safe.

That was her priority – food could wait.

"Shut up, all of you!" barked one of the guards, his voice cold and lacking sympathy. "Dinner was hours ago, and you missed it. Don't expect special treatment."

"Arsehole," the first inmate muttered under her breath.

Kerri bit back a retort, knowing full well that getting on the guard's bad side wouldn't help her situation. Instead, she focused on putting one foot in front of the other, the uncomfortable chains chafing her ankles as she shuffled along.

God, these things are painful!

As they turned a corner, Kerri caught a glimpse of a pale, gaunt face peering out from between the bars of a nearby cell. The defeat in the inmate's eyes chilled her to the bone, serving as a stark reminder of what could possibly be awaiting her within these grim walls.

I can't let this place break me, she told herself as she was marched further along the bleak corridors. *I have to stay strong.*

"Hawthorne, you're in here," the guard said with indifference, unlocking a cell door with a jangling key and then turning to remove her shackles.

Despite her relief in being freed of the chafing metal around her wrists and ankles, Kerri's heart sank as she gazed sadly into her cell. It was a small, dark space with nothing but two hard metal bunks and a narrow slit of a window to let in a sliver of thin moonlight.

Although the feeble glow from the distant overhead light barely illuminated the corners of the cell, as she squinted into the dimness, Kerri discerned the silhouette of another inmate on one of the bunks. The pale moonlight revealed the rhythmic rise and fall of their chest, a telltale sign of someone lost in the realm of sleep. A tentative hope fluttered within Kerri, a wish that this silent cellmate would remain both oblivious and harmless in the encompassing blackness.

"Get in, witch," the guard growled, shoving her roughly inside. "Or I'll make sure this place becomes a living hell for you."

As the cell door was slammed loudly behind her, Kerri's gaze lingered on the unknown sleeper, their dreams unfolding in a parallel world within the claustrophobic embrace of the prison cell.

In the cold, oppressive environment, Kerri leaned against the stone wall, trying to steady herself as the reality of her situation hit her like a tidal wave. Exhausted and with no real choice, she then moved further into the small cell and slumped onto the frigid metal bunk, listening to the echoes of footsteps as they faded down the corridor. She couldn't remember the last time she had felt so tired, or so hungry. Her stomach twisted into knots, a constant reminder that she hadn't eaten all day.

Suddenly, a subtle shift in the shadows of the cell signalled the awakening of Kerri's cellmate. The slow, rhythmic breathing ceased, and was replaced by a gradual stirring that echoed through the confined space.

Kerri's pulse quickened, a silent anxiety threading through her thoughts. She had no idea what to expect, but could only hope that whoever she had woken up wasn't going to be unpleasant about it.

As the sleeper slowly emerged from the cocoon of slumber, Kerri's gaze fixated on her face. The dim light revealed pretty features that seemed, rather than hostile, approachable and unfazed. In that moment, a slight wave of relief washed over Kerri – she sensed her intrusion hadn't roused a potential adversary.

The roused cellmate rubbed her eyes and blinked in the darkness, registering Kerri's presence with a momentary confusion. She then propped herself up on her elbows, causing the thin bedsheet to slip and reveal delicate translucent wings that shimmered a little behind her.

"Hey, you're new, right?"

"Yeah," Kerri replied, trying to muster some enthusiasm, but failing miserably.

"I'm Jayda," the young woman said sleepily, but still with a brightness in her tone. "I've been here for a few months now. It's not so bad, once you get used to it."

"Thanks," Kerri muttered doubtfully, staring at the floor.

"Look, I know it's tough at first," Jayda continued, keen to offer some reassurance, "but most people in here surprise themselves with how well they learn to cope. Besides, I promise I'm a good cellmate."

Kerri knew better than to assume that she could rely on anyone other than her sister. Nevertheless, she couldn't help but admire Jayda's enthusiasm and outgoing demeanour.

"I'm Kerri."

"Pleased to meet you, Kerri," Jayda replied. "What are you in for?"

"It's a long story," Kerri muttered, not particularly eager to recount her mistakes. "What about you?"

"Ah, well, I've got a bit of a habit of taking things that don't belong to me," Jayda confessed with a sheepish grin. "But only small stuff, you know? Nothing too serious."

"You're a thief?" Kerri asked, feeling a shiver run down her spine despite Jayda's seemingly harmless nature.

"Kind of," Jayda said with a shrug. "More like a... collector of lost and forgotten things. But yeah, I guess you could say I'm a thief. Oh, but don't worry – my thieving days are behind me! At least, until I get out of here."

Jayda gave a playful wink, causing Kerri to smile.

"So what are you, exactly?" Kerri asked. "Your wings…"

"Ah! I'm a fae," Jayda explained, twisting around to show off her iridescent wings.

"Interesting," Kerri mused, now more curious than wary of her cellmate.

"Anyhow," said Jayda, "don't stay up all night worrying about stuff. I've already made a few friends around here – well, as friendly as you can get with hardened criminals. I'll be more than happy to introduce you tomorrow."

"Thanks," said Kerri, genuinely grateful.

She still wasn't willing to trust her cellmate entirely, but she very much appreciated Jayda's efforts, especially considering some of the people she had encountered during processing.

"Let's get some rest," said Jayda. "Get some sleep while you can."

"Right," said Kerri.

Sighing heavily, Kerri tried to settle down on the thin metal bed as best as it would allow. As she listened to Jayda's steady breathing, she tried to silence her racing thoughts.

Consumed with worry for Mehgan, she needed to know where they'd taken her, and if she was safe. But how could she possibly find out? The guards would be no help, and neither would the other inmates.

Despite the darkness and the weight of despair that seemed to press down on her chest, Kerri felt a stubborn spark of defiance flickering within. She wasn't going to let this place break her. Not when her sister was here as well.

As she lay there, she made a promise to herself: she would find Mehgan, no matter what it took. And if that meant having to break a few rules, then so be it. Her only option was to use magic – forbidden within these walls, but essential if she wanted any hope of being able to locate her sister.

Kerri knew she had an advantage as a witch; her magic was powerful, and, as long as she used it correctly, discreet. She could use it to locate her sister, but she would have to be careful. One misstep, one careless display of power, and everything could come crashing down around her.

Closing her eyes, Kerri focused on the bond she shared with Mehgan. It was a connection that had always been strong between them, an unbreakable tether that tied their lives together. If she could just tap into that emotional link, then maybe she could locate her sister within the prison.

Drawing in a deep breath, she let the energy flow through her as she crafted a locating spell in her mind. It was a delicate process, like threading a needle in the dark, but she refused to give up. She needed to know that Mehgan was close; that she could still protect her, even from behind bars.

"By blood and bone, by soul and heart," Kerri murmured, her words a barely perceptible whisper. "Guide me to my sister, we can't be apart."

As the spell took hold, a subtle sensation tugged at the edges of Kerri's subconscious. It was faint, but it was there: a compass pointing her in Mehgan's direction. As she followed that invisible thread, relief washed over her like a soothing balm.

Mehgan was nearby. Close enough that Kerri could almost feel her presence, like the softest touch against her skin. Mehgan wasn't out of reach, not yet. The knowledge came to Kerri as a small measure of comfort, a fragile hope that they might find each other again.

Chapter Four

Kerri trailed behind Jayda, the noise of footsteps abundant in the stone-walled corridor.

"Alright," Jayda said, fluttering her delicate wings slightly as she turned around to address Kerri. "Obviously nobody is allowed to use their powers here. That's the official rule from the guards. More than that though, if you absolutely have to do something discreetly, you mustn't do it with the intention of exploiting any inmate. Trust me. It would get you into a whole world of trouble. I've seen it for myself. It never ends well for the perpetrator."

Kerri wanted to ask what had happened, but thought better of it. Besides, there was so much to take in and the hallway was packed with inmates, all making their way down to breakfast.

Kerri's stomach growled as they approached the canteen, hunger gnawing at her insides. The metallic scent of iron mixed with the faint musk of damp and sweat, assaulting her senses as she stepped into the bustling room filled with a mixture of paranormals.

Following Jayda's lead, Kerri grabbed a tray and joined the line. A tall, broad-shouldered woman covered in intricate tattoos stood behind them, her eyes never leaving the back of Kerri's head. Kerri clenched her jaw, deciding that in the volatile environment, she would just have to accept that she was amongst a plethora of personalities – some more challenging than others.

"Another rule for you," said Jayda. "Don't piss off the guards."

Jayda subtly nodded her head towards a muscular woman in uniform standing near the canteen entrance. Kerri noticed the guard shooting a cold glare in the direction of a nearby table of panther shifters.

"Got it," Kerri muttered, still dazed by the unfamiliar and compromising environment.

"Also," Jayda continued, her voice barely audible above the cacophony of clattering cutlery and rowdy conversations, "you're going to need allies. Friends, acquaintances, whatever you want to call them. This place is all about connections, and without them, you're as good as dead."

Kerri raised an eyebrow, wondering how she would ever manage to forge alliances within these walls. However, as her gaze met Jayda's determined eyes, she knew that one person seemed to have her back – at least, as far as other inmates could be trusted.

"Thanks Jayda," Kerri said, picking up a lukewarm bowl of stodgy grey porridge from the counter. "I'll do my best."

Breakfast trays in hand, Kerri and Jayda wove their way through the maze of tables. The din of the built-up area enveloped them as they looked for a place to settle.

Jayda, with a confidence born from familiarity, took the lead, deftly manoeuvring through the ebb and flow of the bustling space. Kerri trailed behind, her steps cautious as she walked through uncharted territory. In their search for a place to sit, the canteen revealed itself as a microcosm of prison life, where something as mundane as where to eat breakfast held significance within the intricate social dynamics of confinement.

"Over there," Jayda said, nodding towards an empty table at the far side of the room.

As Kerri sat down next to Jayda, she noticed that the metal seats, attached firmly to the table, were just as uncomfortable as the metal bunks in their cell. Still though, at least the position of the table provided a perfect vantage point for observation.

"Who are they?" Kerri asked, nodding towards a group of inmates animatedly chatting at a nearby table.

"Those are some of the mages," Jayda replied with a mouthful of porridge, her eyes narrowing as she studied their faces. "Usually harmless, but you never know..."

In the sea of expressive faces, Kerri continued to look for Mehgan, but was having no luck.

I may as well try and get my bearings while I'm here.

"That lot over there," Jayda said quietly as she discretely nodded in the direction of a table in the opposite corner, "are vampires. They're a tricky lot. They might seem quiet, but trust me: they've always got something brewing beneath the surface."

Kerri cautiously took note of the pale-skinned inmates. They lounged languidly in their seats, talking quietly amongst themselves.

"Over there," Jayda whispered, nodding towards a table on the far side of the room. "That's where most of the wolf shifters sit."

Kerri followed Jayda's gaze and saw a group of muscular women huddled together, their expressions guarded and watchful. Their eyes seemed to gleam with an otherworldly light. One thing that stood out about them was the blue armbands made from rags, wrapped around their biceps like makeshift badges of honour.

"What's with their armbands?" Kerri asked, wincing at the particularly cold, hard lump of porridge in her mouth.

"They're the Blue Wolves," Jayda explained, leaning in closer to Kerri so as not to be overheard. "They're one of the more established groups here. They look out for each other, no matter what."

"You're kidding?!" Kerri exclaimed, her eyebrows arching in surprise. "I thought their outside pack alliances would be sacred to them – even in here."

"I can see why you'd think so, but that's the outside world, Kerri. In here, wolf shifters are intense in their kinship. Those who would fight each other to the death on the outside choose to work as allies in here."

"Wow."

"That's wolves for you."

There was a certainty in Jayda's voice that spoke volumes about her own experiences inside. Kerri decided not to pry. Although she was fascinated, she was more concerned about the whereabouts of Mehgan, who she still hadn't managed to spot amongst the crowds huddled all around, despite having sensed that she was nearby last night.

"I'm glad to say that not everyone sticks with

their own kind," Jayda said, her tone optimistic. "It's not all doom and gloom in here. You'll meet some characters though, that's for sure."

Kerri couldn't help but feel amused at Jayda's statement. The fae herself seemed at least a little eccentric. Under the low fluorescent lighting of the canteen, Jayda's long blonde hair, piercing bright eyes, and dynamic expressions conveyed a youthful and optimistic enthusiasm present despite the circumstances.

"Are you gonna eat the rest of that?" Jayda asked hopefully, nodding towards Kerri's porridge.

"You can have it," Kerri answered. "I was so hungry yesterday, but I think I've lost my appetite today."

"It'll come back. The food is awful, but you'll become desensitised to it soon enough."

Kerri had her doubts, but gave a smile all the same.

With their bowls empty, the pair deposited their trays into a hatch, and, under Jayda's lead, made their way to a table close to the canteen's exit.

Kerri could almost taste the tension simmering beneath the surface, an invisible layer of danger that prickled at the back of her neck. As she walked, she felt like a lost prey animal, navigating a forest filled with predators.

With a wave of her hand, Jayda caught the attention of a group of inmates already seated. A varied group of paranormals, they all seemed comfortable in each other's company – there was a panther shifter with eyes that gleamed like polished obsidian, a mage whose fingers seemed to dance with wisps of arcane energy, and a vampire with fangs barely concealed by a tight-lipped smile.

"Hey everyone," said Jayda. "Kerri is my new cellmate. She got here last night."

"Hey Kerri," said the vampire. "I'm Claire."

"Hello," said the mage, raising a hand in greeting. "I'm Rowena."

The panther shifter offered a reluctant smile. Jayda didn't seem to notice, but the cold reception wasn't lost on Kerri.

"Hey Stacey," said Jayda, addressing the

panther shifter. "I'll bring Kerri with us to work in the laundry."

"Suits me," replied the panther shifter, who couldn't have looked more disinterested if she'd tried.

Startling Kerri, a bell rang with an alarming timbre, echoing throughout the canteen. She glanced around, observing the inmates as they began to rise from their seats – some with reluctance, and others with a sense of urgency.

"Right," said Jayda, her tone upbeat and jovial. "Let's get our arses over to the laundry."

Claire and Rowena followed along dutifully after Jayda. Left to walk alongside Stacey, Kerri felt an intensely uncomfortable surge of energy in the air.

"Listen up, witch," Stacey said, leaning in closer to Kerri, her tone low and menacing. "I don't know what kind of magic you've got up your sleeve, but I'm warning you: don't even think about using it on me."

Kerri wanted to tell Stacey to fuck off, but thought better of it. Less than a full day into her prison sentence, she didn't want to make an enemy.

"Hey, no worries," she replied. "I'm not looking for trouble. I just want to keep my head down and serve my time."

"Good," Stacey said, narrowing her eyes, her tone still short and threatening. "Remember that."

Tension coiled within Kerri, the residue of the insulting encounter lingering in the air like an unspoken challenge. The temptation to retaliate tugged at her, but she knew better than to take the bait. Restraining her emotions, she stoically squared her shoulders, an embodiment of resilience in the face of provocation.

Besides, she was still occupied by a more pressing concern.

As she cautiously made her way out of the canteen, she took a last urgent look around the busy space. There was still no sign of Mehgan.

Chapter Five

Keen to avoid Stacey, Kerri caught up with Jayda and stuck with her as the group navigated the dimly lit corridors of the prison. The cold concrete walls seemed to close in on Kerri with every step, but Jayda's warm presence offered a small reprieve from the suffocating atmosphere. As they turned a corner, they were hit with the scent of detergent and damp fabric.

"Here we are," Jayda announced.

Kerri followed her into an expansive room. Bathed in an eerie fluorescent light, the laundry was a cavernous space with rows upon rows of industrial-sized washing machines and dryers. Their low hum droned on, like an army of mechanical cicadas. The air felt heavy with humidity, making it difficult for Kerri to breathe comfortably.

"Damn, this place is huge," she muttered, her voice barely audible over the whir of machinery.

"Yep, lots of dirty clothes to clean," Jayda replied cheerfully. "But don't worry, you'll get used to it."

Kerri sighed, uninspired by the prospect of the task ahead.

"Come on," said Jayda. "Let me introduce you to Tia. She'll show you the ropes."

Jayda then guided Kerri towards a tall, muscular woman, who stood near a table piled high with folded linens.

"Hey, Tia," Jayda called out, waving her hand energetically. "This is Kerri, my new cellmate. She's going to be working with us."

"Nice to meet you, Kerri," Tia said, nodding respectfully. "I've been at this job for a long time, so if you have any questions, don't hesitate to ask."

Tia's voice was gruff, but held a hint of warmth, like a campfire in the dead of winter.

"Thanks," Kerri mumbled, trying to match Tia's tone.

"Alright, let's get started," Tia declared, motioning towards the heaps of dirty laundry waiting to be sorted. "We're responsible for collecting worn clothes and delivering them clean. Do a good job, and maybe one day you'll move up in responsibilities."

Nervously, Kerri nodded her head in compliance. As she picked up a stained vest, she turned to Jayda, who was already sorting through the clothes with practiced efficiency, her wings fluttering rhythmically as she moved.

"I'm pretty fast at this," Jayda announced proudly. "You don't become a thief without learning a thing or two along the way. A good bit of dexterity is everything."

"Were you always a thief?" Kerri asked hesitantly.

Jayda paused, her delicate wings catching the light as she sighed.

"Hmm..." she mused. "I grew up poor and started stealing out of necessity. But after a while... I guess I got addicted to the thrill. And well, here I am."

"Wow," Kerri murmured.

She was taken aback by Jayda's honesty. She felt a pang of sympathy for the fae. They were both trapped within these walls due to their past mistakes.

"Enough about me though," Jayda said with a grin, tossing a pair of socks into a nearby bin before turning to address Tia. "Hey, Tia, the bin's full now. Is it alright if we go out on our round?"

Tia gave a resolute nod, her way of granting permission.

"Right," said Jayda, turning her attention back to Kerri. "Let's get moving."

As they wheeled the laundry cart through the prison, Kerri couldn't shake the nagging feeling that the world outside was slipping further away from her grasp. She desperately hoped that as they manoeuvred around the corridors, perhaps she would see Mehgan. In the comfortable silence as she walked with Jayda, her thoughts became consumed with worry for Mehgan's wellbeing. Mehgan wasn't weak by any means, but that didn't make her absence any easier to bear in a place like this.

"Hey, I'm going to pop to the loo," Kerri said suddenly, noticing a sign for the facilities down a branching corridor. "I'll catch up with you in a bit."

"Alright," Jayda replied. "But don't take too long. This place can be a maze if you're not careful."

Kerri nodded and headed off in the direction of the toilets, leaving the noise of the rattling laundry cart behind her.

As she turned a corner, her ears picked up on a hushed conversation coming from one of the cells. A gut feeling told her to investigate further, even though she knew it might mean trouble. She crept closer to the cell door, pressing her ear against the cold metal surface.

"Listen, you stupid shifter," a male guard's voice taunted in a quiet growl, oozing with menace. "You'd better keep your mouth shut about our little arrangement, or I'll have you beaten so badly that you'll never shift into your wolf form again."

"Fuck you," the wolf shifter retorted, her voice low and gravelly. "You think you can threaten me? I've dealt with worse than you before."

"Is that so?" the guard said with a dark chuckle. "Well, let's see how you feel once you've been beaten into a coma. You'll be stuck in your human form forever, unable to feel the freedom of running on all fours. Remember, I have the power here. Never forget that."

Kerri felt her blood run cold. It was clear to her that a corrupt prison guard was making threats to a fellow inmate. Her heart thundered in her chest, fear mingling with the ever-present sense of injustice that seemed to permeate the prison.

"Piss off," the wolf shifter said with a stubborn growl, her voice barely audible. "Shove your arrangement up your arse. I won't do it."

"That's the wrong answer," the guard replied smugly. "No worries though; I know you'll change your mind. I'll make sure of it."

Kerri pulled away from the cell door as the sound of footsteps approached. Her pulse raced like a hummingbird as she edged away from the cell and quickly down towards the other end of the corridor, the chilling conversation still echoing in her ears. Her thoughts swirled with questions and uncertainty, but she knew one thing for sure: she had stumbled upon something far more sinister than she ever could have anticipated.

"Hey," a smooth voice called out to her.

Kerri stopped dead in her tracks. She turned around to see the wolf shifter stepping confidently out of the cell, her long black hair cascading down her back. Intricate tattoos adorned her arms, telling stories of pain and resilience. The shifter's eyes bored into Kerri's, a fierce intelligence gleaming within their depths.

"I sensed you eavesdropping," the wolf shifter said sternly, a hint of a smirk tugging at the corner of her mouth. "You should know better."

Kerri swallowed, her throat suddenly feeling parched.

"I... I didn't mean to," she stammered, struggling to maintain eye contact with the intimidating woman before her. "I just... I overheard, and I couldn't help it."

"Couldn't help it, huh?" the wolf shifter said as she took a step closer to Kerri, her presence commanding despite her slight frame. "Well, consider this a warning. Don't go poking your nose into other people's business."

Kerri felt her cheeks flush, a mixture of embarrassment and anger at being caught off guard. She had always prided herself on her resourcefulness and her ability to stay one step ahead. This time though, she found herself at a loss for words.

"Look," she finally managed to say, still with a nervous tremble in her voice. "I'm sorry. I was eavesdropping. Yes, I did hear quite a bit, but I swear, I won't do it again and I won't repeat any of this to anyone."

"Good," said the wolf shifter. "Be sure that you don't."

Convinced that the enigmatic woman's tone left no room for further discussion, Kerri decided that she no longer needed to use the loo. Instead, she turned swiftly around and made her way through the dark corridors in search of Jayda.

Chapter Six

The cold metal of the canteen table pressed into Kerri's forearms as she picked at her undercooked baked potato. The beans were watery and tasteless, forming an unappetising puddle on her plate. Only the weak blackcurrant squash was a small reprieve from the bland prison food. She glanced at Jayda, who appeared to be enjoying the meal with her usual bubbly enthusiasm.

As they ate, Stacey sauntered past their table, her long legs moving with predatory grace. Her eyes locked onto Jayda as she offered a friendly nod of greeting. The panther shifter then glared at Kerri, sneering at her with undisguised disdain. Kerri breathed a sigh of relief when Stacey continued on her way to settle down at another table across the room.

"Wow!" Kerri exclaimed quietly. "Stacey really

doesn't like me. I haven't done anything to her. What's her problem?"

"It's nothing personal," Jayda whispered, her delicate wings fluttering slightly as she leaned in closer to Kerri. "Stacey hates all witches. She killed one in self-defence on the outside, or so she claims. Since she got sent to prison, she's been paranoid that all witches are out to get her."

Kerri bit her lip, considering Jayda's words. She made a mental note to keep her distance from Stacey. The last thing she wanted was to make an enemy within these walls. She sensed that Stacey could be very unpleasant if provoked.

I hope Stacey leaves Mehgan alone. I hope I can get to Mehgan first and warn her.

"Thanks for letting me know, Jayda," Kerri said quietly, her mind racing with worry for Mehgan.

"Hey, no worries," said Jayda. "Just keep out of Stacey's way. She's alright with me, but I wouldn't want to get on the wrong side of her."

Kerri nodded, appreciating Jayda's advice.

"Anyway," said Jayda. "I reckon it'll take you a

while to eat your lunch. I'm going to catch up with Claire and Rowena for a bit."

Jayda pointed to a nearby table where the vampire and mage were sitting, engaged in conversation.

Kerri nodded in acknowledgement, and then watched as Jayda bounced her way over to Claire and Rowena. She didn't feel uneasy about being left to sit alone. Besides, most inmates had already finished their meal; there were enough empty seats in the canteen that she would be able to finish her lunch in peace.

Struggling to take another bite of her uninspiring meal, Kerri pushed what was left of her sorry-looking potato around her tray. As she did so, she let her thoughts wander back to what she had witnessed earlier in the corridor. Were all the guards in Grimlock Prison corrupt, or was it an isolated incident?

Although the wolf shifter had told her to mind her own business, Kerri felt worried for her – even though they were practically strangers. She couldn't help but think about what she'd overheard; she wondered what the guard wanted, and was concerned that the wolf shifter was in danger.

She shook her head, trying to rid her mind of the matter; she knew better than to get involved in prison politics. Besides, the need to find Mehgan was far higher on her list of priorities.

Chapter Seven

As several days unfolded in a blur of laundry shifts, unappetising meals, and restless nights, Kerri clung to the hope that she'd find Mehgan.

Sitting at a metal table in the canteen, just as she was staring into space, she was taken aback by the sound of a bell. It echoed through the prison corridors, causing excited chatter to rise amongst the inmates.

"Yes!" Jayda said, dynamically punching the air with her fist. "Yard time!"

The prospect of a brief reprieve from being stuck indoors ignited a spark of hope amongst the prisoners. Even the moodiest amongst them seemed a little lighter in their step as they made their way towards the yard.

Kerri's heart skipped a beat; it wasn't so much the offer of fresh air that gave her a flicker of optimism, but the thought of finally finding Mehgan. The promise of yard time held the potential for a long-awaited reunion. If Mehgan was indeed in the same wing, this could be their moment.

With hoards of other orange-clad inmates, Kerri stepped out into the yard with a glimmer of expectation. Amidst the shuffling footsteps and the ambient hum of anticipation, her hope of spotting Mehgan transcended the harsh reality of incarceration.

Kerri looked around, her face a picture of focus and determination. The yard was filled with paranormals of every kind – mages, vampires, fae, wolf shifters, panther shifters, and witches – all either huddled together in cliques, or mingling freely among one another. Kerri scanned the sea of faces, searching for any sign of her sister, but the sheer volume of people made it nearly impossible.

Although the warm afternoon sun was undeniably pleasant, Kerri knew that she wouldn't have long to find Mehgan. With a purposeful stride, she began to weave her way through the crowd, her eyes darting from one group to another. She felt a surge of frustration as the minutes ticked by and yard time began to wane.

"Excuse me," she muttered as she urgently made her way through the maze of groups and individuals dotted about.

As she continued to cover ground, Kerri suddenly found herself face-to-face with Stacey. The air thickened with tension as their eyes locked in a silent clash of animosity. Stacey's lips curled into a sneer, her predatory gaze fixed on Kerri.

"Well, well, if it isn't the little witch," she taunted, her words slicing through the yard's ambience.

Kerri, taken aback but refusing to show weakness, squared her shoulders.

"Stacey," she replied evenly, her voice deliberately in contrast to the charged atmosphere.

Without warning, Stacey purposefully shoulder-barged into Kerri. The collision was both physical and symbolic – a calculated move that screamed blind hatred. She then quickly stepped back, feigning naivety with a malicious glint in her eyes.

"Oops, clumsy me," she mocked, a façade of innocence masking the true intent behind her actions.

"Can you please move?" Kerri asked, trying to keep her voice steady, not wishing to take the bait.

Stacey stood firm, blocking Kerri's path and smirking at her obvious irritation.

"Make me," she challenged, crossing her arms and daring Kerri to retaliate.

In that moment, something snapped inside Kerri. Maybe it was the mounting pressure to find Mehgan, or perhaps it was just the sheer audacity of Stacey. Whatever it was, it propelled her forward as she grabbed Stacey's shoulders and tried to shove her out of the way.

The courtyard erupted into chaos as the two women grappled, their fight drawing a circle of onlookers eager to witness the spectacle. No shifting occurred and no magic was used. Instead, they fought ruggedly, nails digging into flesh, and fists flying.

"Is this what you want, Stacey?" Kerri said through clenched teeth. "Are you really so petty?"

"Fuck you, witch," Stacey replied with a snarl, her hand tightening its grip around Kerri's hair.

As the scuffle continued, Kerri knew she was fighting a losing battle, but still she refused to back down. She had to find Meghan – and if that meant standing up to a panther shifter with a vendetta against witches, so be it.

"You witches think you're untouchable," Stacey uttered, a panther's growl beneath her words.

They grappled in a dance of mutual disdain, each refusing to concede. Yet, in the relentless push and pull, Kerri sensed the tide turning.

Stacey, a whirlwind of feral strength, executed a final, ruthless move. With calculated precision, she swept Kerri's legs from beneath her, sending her tumbling towards the unforgiving concrete.

Sprawled out on the ground, her head spinning from the impact, as Kerri blinked through the haze, she saw a familiar face hovering above her, concern etched across her features.

"Mehgan?!" she exclaimed, her voice a mixture of surprise and relief as her sister bent down towards her, a guardian in the midst of the mayhem.

"Are you ok?" Mehgan asked, her tone cutting through the lingering tension like a lifeline.

"I think so," Kerri replied, still dazed.

Reaching down to grab Kerri by the arms, Mehgan helped her to her feet.

Before they could say anything more, a guard appeared, marching towards Kerri with a stern expression.

"You!" he barked. "Fighting is against the rules. Come with me. You're going to solitary confinement."

As the guard roughly grabbed her by the arm and began to lead her away, Kerri stole one last glance at Mehgan. It devastated her that their reunion had been cut so damn short.

***

The journey to solitary confinement was a blur of twisting corridors and heavy metal doors. Kerri's heart pounded in time with the guard's heavy footsteps as they echoed through the dark, damp halls. Her frustration simmered beneath the surface, threatening to bubble over. How had everything gone so wrong?

When they finally reached the solitary confinement cell, the guard forced Kerri inside with a firm shove. She stumbled forward, and before she had regained her composure, she heard the door clang shut behind her.

Alone in the tiny, oppressive space, the walls seemed to close in on Kerri, the air thick and stagnant. She had no choice but to sink onto the hard cot that served as the cell's only furniture. Her body aching from the fight, she was hit by a stark blend of anger and despair.

Chapter Eight

The relentless discomfort of solitary confinement gnawed at Kerri's sanity, the time stretching into a seemingly endless abyss. The tiny cell was her entire world now, the damp floors and walls restraining her, suffocating her with each passing moment. The cot that served as a bed was close to useless, providing little comfort from the cold concrete beneath. Sleep seemed like a luxury that she would never enjoy again.

Her stomach churned with hunger, the sporadic and meagre meals barely sustaining her. She wondered how long it had been since she had seen her sister in the yard, her worried expression etched into her memory. As minutes blurred into hours, and hours into days, Kerri felt herself slipping, her thoughts growing darker and more desperate. The oppression weighed heavily on her chest, as if the very shadows were trying to smother her.

Lying on her back on the frigid, hard cot, her long dark hair fanned out around her face, her expression remaining tense. She wanted to sleep, not just due to exhaustion, but because it would help pass the time. However, even the tormenting silence of solitary confinement seemed to make sleep feel impossible.

As she tossed and turned, seeking even a moment's respite from her thoughts, a sound pierced the quietness. It was the unmistakable sound of someone sobbing. It seemed to be coming from the cell next to Kerri's.

She hesitated, wondering if it was wise to draw attention to herself, but ultimately, her innate compassion won out over self-preservation.

"Hey, are you ok?" she called out cautiously, her voice barely more than a whisper.

"Fuck off," came the curt response, tinged with pain and frustration.

I recognise that voice! It's the wolf shifter who had a go at me for eavesdropping!

Despite the harsh words, there was something inside Kerri that refused to be put off. She thought back to the wolf shifter's wary eyes and the hint of vulnerability that had been carefully masked behind a tough exterior. It had now been replaced by raw emotion that echoed against the concrete walls. Even though they were strangers, Kerri felt a deep-rooted sense of empathy for the woman and an urge to offer comfort.

"Hey, I'm sorry," Kerri whispered sincerely. "I just thought... maybe you could use someone to talk to."

The only response was the continued sound of muffled crying.

"Look, I'm not judging you for crying," Kerri said gently, authenticity in her tone. "We all need someone to talk to sometimes, especially in this hellhole. If you change your mind, I'm here."

"Maybe talking would help to pass the time," the wolf shifter admitted, sounding slightly less hostile.

"Alright then," Kerri replied, sitting up on her cot and tugging at the frayed edges of her vest. "Tell me something about yourself – anything, really."

Despite her caution, Kerri sensed that the wolf shifter needed a lifeline. Besides, for her own benefit, she yearned to quash the tedium of solitary.

"Ok," said the wolf shifter, now with a slight playfulness in her tone. "I used to love running through the woods when I was younger, especially during a full moon. It felt... freeing."

Kerri smiled faintly, envisioning a lithe, feral creature darting through the shadows, guided by moonlight and instinct.

"That sounds incredible," she said wistfully. "I always loved being out in nature. My sister and I would often go on hikes together."

"I'm Sammi, by the way," said the wolf shifter.

"Pleased to properly meet you. I'm Kerri."

"Cool," said Sammi. "And I'm sorry about the other day when I had a go at you. It's just that... I've got some shit going on with one of the guards at the moment. It's messy as fuck."

"Oh," Kerri murmured in response, not quite sure what to say, but sensing that she mustn't pry.

"You seem alright, Kerri. Just take my word for it when I say that you want to avoid Officer Crowley at all costs."

"Is that the guard who was threatening you?"

The conversation came to an uncomfortable pause. Kerri could have kicked herself for having been so nosy.

"Sorry, Sammi," she said. "I shouldn't have asked."

"It's ok. There's nothing anyone can do to help me. I'm fucked either way."

Beneath Sammi's tough exterior, Kerri sensed that the wolf shifter needed a friend.

"It sounds like you're in deep with something horrible," Kerri said.

"Big time," Sammi answered. "Crowley is going to make my life a living hell, and there's nothing I can do about it."

Chapter Nine

"Shit! Someone's coming!" Sammi said suddenly, her voice a mixture of panic and frustration.

The unmistakable sound of heavy boots echoed from a nearby corridor, announcing the imminent arrival of a guard. Kerri was certain that it was too early for anyone to be bringing food. She panicked; she didn't want to interact with the guards unless she absolutely had to. Without hesitation, she curled up on her cot, feigning sleep whilst fully alert.

Facing the near wall with her eyes closed, she focused on her breathing. The footsteps grew louder until they stopped right outside Sammi's cell. As the door creaked open, Kerri strained to catch every word of conversation.

"Changed your mind yet?" the guard said

mockingly, his voice low and threatening.

"Please, I can't do it," Sammi begged, trying to sound defiant but her voice betraying her fear. "I can't kill anyone. I'm not a murderer."

"You've got two options," the guard replied coldly. "Accept my offer of parole in exchange for taking out my man on the outside, or rot in this hellhole. I'd choose wisely if I were you."

In response to hearing this, Kerri's stomach clenched. She silently cursed herself for eavesdropping, but she couldn't help it. What kind of monster would force someone into such a horrific dilemma?

"Think about it," the guard continued, his voice dripping with menace. "I trust you'll make the right decision for both of us."

The sound of heavy boots retreated, leaving Sammi's desperate sobs in their wake. Kerri remained quiet until the guard had long gone, but thereafter, she couldn't stand it anymore. She sat up and spoke quietly to Sammi.

"Was that Officer Crowley? The corrupt guard you mentioned?"

"Yeah," Sammi uttered with a sniffle, struggling to stifle a sob. "That was him."

"Look, I heard everything," Kerri admitted, feeling a wave of guilt wash over her.

"Kerri," Sammi whispered, her voice quivering with a combination of fear and anger. "Crowley wants me to kill someone on the outside. He's in debt to a wolf shifter, and he wants me to take them out."

Kerri's heart pounded in her chest as she tried to process the horrifying information.

"Sammi… that's… that's terrible. Have you ever killed anyone?"

"Of course not!" Sammi snapped, sounding almost offended by the question. "I'm in Grimlock because I beat-up a wolf shifter who was bullying a cub. But murder? No fucking way! That's not me at all."

"Then why not lie to Crowley?" Kerri suggested, her mind racing for a solution. "Tell him you'll do what he wants, get your parole, and then just run far away. Start over somewhere else."

"Are you kidding?" Sammi scoffed. "If I double-cross Crowley, I'd be looking over my shoulder for the rest of my life. He'd never stop hunting me down."

Kerri wrung her hands together, feeling utterly helpless.

"What about the Blue Wolves in here?" she asked. "Could you reach out to them for help?"

"Kerri, I've always been a lone wolf," Sammi explained, her voice laced with a hint of pride. "Trying to buddy up with the Blue Wolves now would look as fake as anything. Besides, I doubt they'd want to get involved in something so damn messy."

"What are you going to do?" Kerri asked, concern evident in her tone.

"I don't know," Sammi admitted, her voice barely above a whisper. "I just... I don't know."

"I wish there was something I could do to help," said Kerri.

Although she didn't know Sammi well, Kerri meant every word. She knew that if one inmate was vulnerable to the ways of Officer Crowley, then it could be any of them having to face similar problems later down the line.

"Hey, you're a witch, right?" Sammi said, a glimmer of hope in her tone. "Couldn't you just, I don't know, put a spell on Officer Crowley or something?"

Kerri knew that using her magic was what had landed her in this hellhole in the first place. The last thing she wanted was to make things worse for herself, or for Mehgan. As much as she wanted to protect Sammi, she couldn't risk it.

"Sammi, I can't," Kerri said, her words heavy with regret. "My magic is what got me sent here in the first place. I can't take the risk, not when it could jeopardise my chances of getting out. Besides, I've got Mehgan to think about – my sister. We came in together, and we're leaving together."

"Your sister..." Sammi murmured, understanding dawning in her voice. "Yeah, I get it. Family's important."

"More than anything," Kerri agreed, a bittersweet smile tugging at the corners of her lips.

They sat quietly for a while, separated by the unforgiving concrete wall. Kerri felt an ache deep within her chest, the unfairness of it all threatening to consume her.

Chapter Ten

The harsh sunlight glinted off the walls of the prison yard, casting jagged shadows on the cracked concrete. Kerri squinted against the brightness, her heart aching with sympathy for Sammi. She could still hear the haunted tone in Sammi's voice echoing in her mind from their quiet conversations in solitary confinement. But now was not the time to dwell on that; she needed to find Mehgan and steer clear of Stacey.

Kerri pulled her collar up to shield her neck from the sun as she scanned the yard. She took measured steps in a careful effort to avoid drawing attention to herself. It was crucial to maintain a low profile, especially after her altercation with Stacey. She strategically flicked her gaze over the clusters of prisoners enjoying their brief time outdoors.

Kerri heard Mehgan's laughter before spotting her.

Mehgan's hanging out with the Blue Wolves?!

Kerri's pulse quickened as she thought back to Jayda's warning about this gang, comprised mainly of hardened wolf shifters who stuck together like glue. Could Mehgan really be associating with them?

"Kerri!" Mehgan called out, waving her over.

At first, Kerri was gripped by a moment of hesitation, but it soon melted away as her need to reconnect with her sister won out. With a burst of determination, she darted through the crowd towards Mehgan.

"Hey," Kerri said breathlessly as she approached.

"Kerri! I missed you. It's so good to see that you're out of solitary," Mehgan said, her expression a picture of relief. "Let's walk."

With a swift nod at the Blue Wolves, Mehgan excused herself, and then moved to link arms with Kerri.

As they strolled along the edge of the yard, Kerri stole a glance back at the Blue Wolves.

"I've come to realise that we only get yard time together," said Mehgan. "The prison's scheduling is a nightmare; you and I both work and eat at different times, but everyone on this wing gets yard time together."

"That's such a relief," said Kerri. "I don't know how I'd cope if we were in different wings. Thank fuck for yard time."

"That reminds me," said Mehgan, a smirk tugging at her lips. "Unlike your last time out here, I don't think Stacey will be giving you any more trouble."

"Oh?" Kerri uttered, unsure of what Mehgan was getting at, but deeply curious all the same.

Mehgan giggled, a mischievous glint in her eyes. She then lowered her voice and leaned in closer to Kerri.

"While you were in solitary, I made sure to get a little revenge. I cast a discreet spell to make Stacey's feet swell up like balloons. She was practically waddling in her shoes for two days straight."

"You used magic? Mehgan, you know we're not supposed to..."

"I wasn't going to let Stacey bully you, or any other witch," Mehgan said with a resolute look, unapologetically cutting Kerri off. "Sometimes, you have to break a few rules."

Kerri sighed, torn between worry and understanding.

"But using magic?" she insisted. "You know that's against the rules here."

"It was worth it. Stacey might know it was me, but now she's backed off from picking on other witches too."

"What if she finds out for certain it was you, and decides to come after you?" Kerri asked, her features etched with concern.

Mehgan shrugged, a newfound confidence emanating from her.

"I've been getting respect from the Blue Wolves," she said. "Standing up against a bully does wonders for your prison cred. I've moved up the ranks a bit."

Kerri, taken aback, studied her sister.

"Mehgan, you never struck me as rebellious. Just be careful. You don't want to make enemies with the wrong person."

"Don't worry, I've got this," Mehgan said, a confident sparkle in her eyes. "Anyway, tell me about solitary. What was it like?"

"It was dark and damp," Kerri confessed. "The food was worse than what we get in the canteen, and the bed... well, calling it a bed would be generous."

"That sounds horrible."

"It was," Kerri admitted. "If it wasn't for Sammi being in the cell next to mine, I could have easily gone out of my mind. We couldn't see each other, but we could talk."

"Sammi? The wolf shifter? I think I've seen her around."

"Yeah."

"It sounds like solitary might have been a nice little holiday for you," Mehgan said with a chuckle, trying to lighten the mood. "I mean, Sammi is your type, isn't she?"

Kerri couldn't deny it. Heat rushed to her cheeks.

"Yeah, she's my type," she said softly, her eyes downcast. "But it's not that. She's in trouble. Officer Crowley is trying to blackmail her into killing someone for him on the outside."

"What?!" Mehgan exclaimed, her expression turning serious and her playful demeanour vanishing. "Are you kidding?"

"I wish I was," Kerri replied grimly. "I want you to avoid Officer Crowley at all costs, Mehgan. I mean it. He's dangerous."

"Does anyone else know about this?" Mehgan asked, her brow furrowing with concern.

"Only Crowley, Sammi, me, and now you," Kerri said. "And I need you to keep it that way."

"Too bad the Blue Wolves don't know," Mehgan mused. "They wouldn't let a fellow shifter be exploited like that."

"Please, Mehgan," Kerri urged. "I need you to promise me that you won't tell anyone what I've just told you."

"Alright," Mehgan agreed after a moment's pause. "I promise."

"Thank you," said Kerri, breathing a sigh of relief.

She didn't like the thought of Mehgan getting too close to the Blue Wolves. A witch in a gang of wolf shifters would always be the odd one out.

As the sisters continued their walk, the sun dipped a little lower in the sky, casting long shadows across the yard. For a brief moment, Kerri tried to forget they were trapped within the walls of a prison for paranormals, bound by rules and watched by enemies. Much to her disappointment though, as the bell signalling the end of yard time rang out, she was soon brought crashing back down to reality.

"Stay safe, sis," said Kerri, unable to hide the emotion in her voice.

"You too," Mehgan whispered.

They shared a final hug before parting ways, each lost in their own thoughts as they returned to their respective corners of the wing.

Kerri admired Mehgan's newfound strength and courage. It pleased her that her sister was able to stand up for herself. Still though, as Kerri made her way back to the laundry for work, her mind buzzed with the intensity of all they had discussed.

Chapter Eleven

As the prison settled into the hushed embrace of evening lockdown, Kerri lay on her bunk, her eyes fixed on the unforgiving expanse of the concrete ceiling. Shadows flickered against its stark surface, casting a web of reflection that mimicked the intricate tapestry of her thoughts.

"…and then," Jayda said, stifling a giggle, "Rowena accidentally dropped an entire bottle of bleach into the washer! It looked like a snowstorm had exploded inside!"

Kerri mumbled incoherently, her response noncommittal and disinterested.

"Come on, Kerri," said Jayda. "Lighten up."

Not wishing to alienate her cellmate, Kerri made the effort to sit up, but still her engagement was minimal. She stared blankly at her hands and picked at a loose thread on one of her sleeves.

Evidently frustrated that Kerri hadn't seen the humour in her recollection of laundry mishaps, Jayda let out a sigh.

"Hey," she said softly, tilting her head. "What's wrong?"

"It's just... I've been out of solitary for a week now, and I still haven't seen Sammi," said Kerri, her eyes dark with worry as she met Jayda's gaze. "She's been in there longer than anyone else has since I arrived at Grimlock. It doesn't feel right."

"You're right, it is strange," said Jayda, frowning, and nodding in agreement. "There are only so many cells in solitary confinement. The prison can't keep people in there forever; they need at least a few cells to be available in order to maintain control. They rely on being able to threaten everyone with an immediate trip to solitary at any moment."

As Jayda spoke, Kerri's mind raced. The implication of this information was clear: Sammi was in serious trouble. Officer Crowley was probably going out of his way to keep her in solitary for as long as possible. The thought caused anger and dread to surge through Kerri's veins, but she knew she couldn't share the details with Jayda – not without putting Sammi in even more danger.

"Something's wrong," Kerri murmured, swallowing hard. "I just think it's awful how Sammi is being kept in solitary for so long."

Jayda reached over, placing a comforting hand on Kerri's arm.

"Come on, Kerri," she said with a playful grin. "Perhaps Sammi's time in solitary is grating on you because you miss her. I'd even go so far as to say you fancy her, don't you?"

Kerri couldn't help but laugh at the absurdity of the situation.

"Ok, fine," she admitted, her cheeks flushing with warmth. "I can't deny that I like being around Sammi, but let's get real here: I'm not going to entertain the idea of a prison romance. I need to focus on getting out; Mehgan and I came in here together, sisters united, and that's how we're leaving."

"Fair enough," Jayda said, still smiling.

***

The next day, during yard time, Kerri eagerly scanned the bustling crowd for Mehgan. When she finally spotted her, she made her way through the throng of inmates, relief washing over her when they embraced.

"I see you've been hanging out with the Blue Wolves again," Kerri remarked, her voice tinged with concern.

"Yeah," said Mehgan. "They may be tough, but they're straight-talking and more fun than most people in here. And I know they respect me."

Kerri hesitated, but decided to trust her sister's judgment. If anyone could handle herself among this domineering group, it was Mehgan – if only based on her recent conduct.

As they stood beside each other, Mehgan noticed Kerri's thoughtful expression.

"What's up?" she asked. "Talk to me about it."

Kerri recounted the conversation she'd had with

Jayda about Sammi's extended stay in solitary confinement. As she spoke, worry etched lines of concern on her forehead, her eyes betraying a sense of helplessness that gnawed at her core.

Mehgan, having listened carefully and diligently taken in every detail, took a deep breath before giving Kerri a considered response.

"Ok. I hear you," she said. "You might not like what I've got to say about this, but I don't want to bullshit you either, Kerri. The way I see it, is that you've only got two options: You can either stop worrying about Sammi, or take action to help her. There's literally nothing else you can do."

Taken slightly aback by her sister's blunt advice, Kerri had no time to dwell on it.

"Let me introduce you to some of the Blue Wolves," Mehgan insisted. "Regardless of what you're going to do in here, you need allies."

"Are you sure?" Kerri asked cautiously.

"Yes," Mehgan urged. "You'll never make it through our sentence if you're constantly worrying."

With a sigh, Kerri allowed Mehgan to lead her over to the group of Blue Wolves who lounged against one of the yard walls, their body language exuding confidence and strength. As the sisters approached, the gang members eyed Kerri with curiosity, sizing her up.

"Hey everyone," Mehgan called out, gaining the group's attention. "This is my sister, Kerri. She's cool, so I thought I'd introduce her to you all."

"Hey Kerri," said one of the Blue Wolves, extending a tattooed hand in greeting. "I'm Lark. Good to meet you."

"Thanks," Kerri mumbled, taking Lark's hand and giving it a firm shake.

Lark's grip, strong and assured, conveyed a sense of authority, her calloused fingers a testament to a life defined by the harsh realities of incarceration and other unspoken hardships. Towering and muscular, she exuded an air of undeniable resilience. Her eyes, sharp and observant, hinted at a complex amalgamation of toughness and reason.

There was something about the way the Blue Wolves carried themselves that made Kerri feel both intimidated and intrigued. Their presence, like a current beneath the surface, seemed to dominate within the dynamics of the prison. Although the mere mention of the Blue Wolves sent ripples all around – an enigma that commanded both respect and stirred the currents – Kerri couldn't deny her cautious fascination.

I trust Mehgan's judgement. If the Blue Wolves have been alright with her, then perhaps they're not as difficult as their reputation implies.

Kerri didn't doubt that she wouldn't want to be on the wrong side of the Blue Wolves, but all the same, there was no denying that any one of them could prove to be useful as an ally.

Chapter Twelve

The wheels of the laundry cart squeaked and groaned as Kerri and Jayda shuffled through the dimly lit prison corridors. Jayda, her delicate wings shimmering in the faint light, filled the silence with her bubbly chatter. Even in a place like Grimlock Prison, she somehow managed to find reasons to smile.

Despite the worries that plagued her mind, Kerri couldn't help but enjoy Jayda's company. Her vivacious nature seemed to have an infectious impact. However, her playful banter was cut short by a sudden sound that pierced the air; someone nearby was sobbing.

Kerri's breath hitched as she recognised the pain in those cries. As she and Jayda wheeled the laundry cart along, they followed the sorrowful sound. It led them to a stop at Sammi's cell. As they stood outside and peered in, they saw the wolf shifter sitting on her bunk. She was hunched over, the tremble in her shoulders portraying her distress.

It broke Kerri's heart to see Sammi so defeated.

Sensing Kerri's concern, Jayda gave her a knowing look.

"I'll leave you two alone," she whispered tactfully.

As Jayda headed off down the corridor with the laundry cart, Kerri stepped into the cell and quietly sat down next to Sammi on the hard metal bed.

"Sammi?" she coaxed softly.

At the sound of Kerri's voice, Sammi slowly lifted her head from her trembling hands. Her eyes were swollen and bloodshot. Tears ran in glistening trails down her puffy cheeks. Her face was a canvas of pain and suffering, her delicate features marred by angry red marks and dark bruises. Kerri's shock and dismay at the sight quickly turned into a raging anger.

"Who did this to you?" she demanded, her voice

shaking with disgust.

"Who do you think?" Sammi replied bitterly, hoarse from crying.

"It was that bastard Crowley, wasn't it?" Kerri said, clenching her fists.

Sammi nodded her head in shame, her eyes dark with defeat.

"He got me while I was in solitary, when all of the other cells were empty. He must have been waiting for the right moment."

"Bastard," said Kerri, aching at the thought of Sammi having been so helpless.

"I would have shifted into my wolf form to defend myself," Sammi admitted, "but after fuck knows how many weeks in solitary, I was too weak and hungry. I couldn't shift."

"By my count, you were in there for around three weeks – give or take a bit," said Kerri.

"Fuck!" Sammi replied. "It felt much longer."

"I bet."

Sammi looked at Kerri with an almost grateful expression in her gaze. Not all prisoners taken to solitary confinement had someone in the main prison population counting down the days until their release.

Suddenly, the sound of heavy boots echoed from further down the corridor, causing Kerri to shudder with unease. She was supposed to be working, and if caught without the laundry cart, she'd be in trouble.

A quick glance at Sammi's battered face solidified Kerri's resolve. With a whispered promise to return, she slipped behind the open door of Sammi's cell, her heart pounding as she waited for the guard to pass. She pressed herself against the cold concrete wall, her breath catching in the claustrophobic space behind the slightly ajar door.

The plan had been simple: to wait for the guard to pass by. Yet, as she stood silently in the narrow space, dread clawed at her when the footsteps in the corridor took an unexpected turn and entered the cell. Kerri could only listen from behind the door, and pray that she wouldn't be spotted.

"You pathetic piece of shit," mocked the unmistakable voice of Officer Crowley as he addressed Sammi. "Are you so stupid that you still refuse to make the right choice?"

Powerless and afraid to do anything other than remain hidden, Kerri's blood ran cold as she took in the spiteful words.

"Please," Sammi begged, her voice trembling, desperation evident in her tone. "I won't do it. I can't."

"Wrong answer," Crowley said with a malicious growl. "I'll see to it that you rot in this hellhole until you realise your only choice is to agree to my deal. Just agree to kill my man on the outside, and you get parole. Simple as that."

Kerri's fists clenched involuntarily as Officer Crowley's taunts sliced through the air. Every venomous word from his mouth felt like a strike against not just Sammi, but against the very core of her own restraint. The desire to rush to Sammi's side battled against the rational acknowledgment of the risks that defiance would present in this unforgiving environment.

The urge to unleash her magic against the

corrupt prison officer surged within, a visceral response to the injustice of it all. Kerri yearned to stop Crowley, to wield her supernatural abilities as a shield against the cruelty. Yet, a harsh reality grounded her; using her magic – or indeed, getting involved at all – would probably escalate the situation. Not only would Kerri get herself in trouble, but her actions would probably result in Sammi being subjected to even harsher consequences.

Snapping Kerri out of her whirling thoughts, a choked cry escaped Sammi as the sharp sound of a violent blow filled the air. Kerri's eyes widened in horror as her chest tightened with a blend of fury and fear. The attack had been vicious but swift, just enough to keep Sammi in her place without attracting attention.

"You'd better start thinking about this properly," Officer Crowley said with a threatening snarl.

With that, he stormed out of the cell, his boots echoing down the corridor as he walked away.

Standing in shock, and still in her hiding place, Kerri listened as the fading footsteps marked the exit of Sammi's tormentor. In the lingering atmosphere of tension, Sammi's stifled sobs and trembling breaths replaced the abrasive tone of Crowley's taunts, a haunting aftermath of the encounter.

As soon as the coast was clear, Kerri stepped out from behind the door, aching at the sight of Sammi curled up on the hard bed, fresh tears streaming down her bruised face. Without hesitation, Kerri wrapped her arms around the poor wolf shifter, offering a protective embrace. Sammi clung to her, gasping sobs causing her whole body to shake.

"Sammi, I'm so sorry," Kerri whispered, the rage simmering within every fibre of her being.

As she tried to offer solace to Sammi, Kerri couldn't ignore the harsh reality of how their shared vulnerability lingered in the air. The walls of the cell seemed to close in on them, a suffocating reminder of the powerlessness that defined their existence.

Chapter Thirteen

Kerri's leg bounced under the canteen table, her impatience growing with every passing second. She glanced at the clock, her heart racing as she counted down the minutes to yard time. She needed to tell Mehgan everything that had been going on; her worries were festering inside her like a wound, threatening to consume her.

"Yard time!" the guard barked in response to the loud ringing of the prison bell.

Finally! thought Kerri. She bolted from her seat, the stiff metal creaking beneath her weight as she moved. Ignoring the annoyed glares from the other inmates, she pushed through the throng of bodies, her eyes already scanning for her sister outside.

As she stepped into the yard, the sun beat down

on her face, warming her skin. The air buzzed with the energy of pent-up emotions, the prisoners forming their own clusters across the dusty ground. And there, leaning against the far fence, was Mehgan. She was with the Blue Wolves again. Their respect for her was evident in the way they gave her space, nodding their heads in deference as she spoke.

"Mehgan!" Kerri called out, her voice barely audible above the din of the yard.

Mehgan looked up, and, recognising the urgency in her sister's expression, excused herself from the group conversation.

"Hey Kerri," she said thoughtfully, her eyes filled with concern.

They moved to the edge of the yard, where the noise was somewhat muffled by the towering concrete walls surrounding them.

"You look ever so worked-up," Mehgan observed. "What's wrong?"

"Sammi's out of solitary," Kerri blurted, unable to contain her emotions any longer. "But it's fucking awful, Mehgan. Officer Crowley beat her up. Not only did he have a go at her in solitary, but he went for her yesterday; when I visited Sammi in her cell, Crowley barged in and started being violent with her. I didn't see anything because I hid behind the door when we heard him coming, but I heard everything. It was relentless."

A shudder rippled through Kerri's body as the memory replayed vividly in her mind.

"Fuck," Mehgan whispered, her expression darkening with a blend of anger and fear.

"I'm so worried about Sammi," said Kerri, her voice shaking. "It's not just that though; if Crowley can do that to one prisoner, he can do it to any of us. I mean, who's to say that he wouldn't go for me or you? We're due out in six months; what if he's in the habit of threatening prisoners due for release to do his dirty work on the outside?!"

Kerri looked into her sister's eyes, pleading for understanding.

"Six months?" Mehgan mused, confusion furrowing her brow. "Kerri, our sentence is three years. Two and a half for arson, and another six months on top of that as punishment for what it will cost the city for the library repairs."

"Wh… what?!" Kerri stammered, her heart sinking like a stone in her chest. "I thought we were both given six months?!"

"I guess you were too shocked to take it all in. We were sentenced to three years, Kerri. I'm sure of it."

"Are you?" Kerri asked, her tone rising in disbelief.

"Hmm..." Mehgan mused hesitantly. "I was in shock too, but I distinctly remember the judge saying three years in total."

"But what if *you* misheard?" Kerri reasoned, doubt and desperation clawing at her train of thought.

"I don't know," Mehgan replied, mirroring Kerri's uncertainty. "Perhaps I did. We must have both replayed that moment in our heads so many times by now. It's understandable that our memories of it could have become distorted along the way."

"Ok," said Kerri, hit by a sudden burst of inspiration. "Let's think rationally about this. We can't trust any of the guards to give us the clarification we need. None of them care about us. We'll have to do this our own way."

"What do you mean?" Mehgan asked, suspiciously raising an eyebrow.

"I'll do it tonight: I'm going to use a discreet spell to locate our sentence file," Kerri insisted, a glimmer of determination in her eyes. "Jayda's a deep sleeper; I can work my magic without being caught."

***

Locked down for the night, Kerri listened as the sounds of the prison gradually quietened. She waited for what felt like an eternity until she was certain that Jayda had fallen into a deep sleep, the fae's gentle snores mingling with the distant murmurs of other inmates.

Taking a deep breath as she lay on her bunk, Kerri clasped her hands together, murmuring a spell under her breath. As the words left her lips, she felt a wave of energy surging through her body, heightening her senses and connecting her to the unseen world beyond the prison walls. Within her mind's eye, she delved into the depths of the courtroom records, searching for that one crucial file that held the truth about her and Mehgan's sentence.

At last, she found it: a dusty, worn folder marked with their names. She hesitated for a moment, her pulse racing in anticipation, before carefully opening the file in her mind. A sickening knot formed in her stomach as she read the judge's ruling: three years imprisonment – two and a half for arson, and an additional six months for the cost of repairing the city library.

"Fuck," she whispered, tears prickling at the corners of her eyes.

With the vital information in hand, she allowed the spell to dissipate. As the magic eased from her mind and the painful truth hit her hard, she was left with a cold, empty feeling inside. She shivered as the reality of their situation bore down on her like a crushing weight.

Three years. Three long, agonising years, trapped within the relentless, unforgiving walls of Grimlock Prison. She'd been so sure, so certain, that it would only be six months. But

Mehgan had been right all along. How could she have been so naive?

As the enormity of their predicament settled in, Kerri couldn't hold back the tears any longer. They flowed silently down her cheeks, dripping onto the hard metal below as she curled up on her bunk, trying to find some semblance of comfort in the darkness. Sleep, however, remained elusive, taunting her with dreams of freedom just beyond her reach.

***

In her need to talk to Mehgan, the anticipation during the build-up to yard time had clawed at Kerri's nerves. Finally, she found herself outside, appreciative of the fresh afternoon air despite how being granted access to it wasn't her most pressing concern.

The vast expanse of the yard buzzed with activity as inmates mingled, their voices forming a cacophony that underscored the acute urgency of Kerri's priorities.

Spotting Mehgan amidst the bustling sea of inmates, she hurriedly approached, desperation etched on her face.

Mehgan excused herself from the conversation she had been engaged in, urgency mirrored in her eyes as she joined Kerri for a private discussion. They then proceeded to walk the perimeter of the yard, the weight of worry hanging heavily between them.

"Did you do it?" Mehgan asked, the pressing need in her voice cutting through the air.

Kerri nodded, a heavy sigh escaping her lips.

"Yes," she said. "You were right, Mehgan. It's three years, not six months."

"I thought so," Mehgan confirmed, her expression betraying her disappointment.

"It has given me a lot to think about," said Kerri. "There I was thinking that we had to keep to ourselves and keep out of trouble for just six months. Although it sounded hard, it seemed *possible*. But three years, Mehgan? Three fucking years?!"

"I know," said Mehgan, her tone laced with sadness and defeat.

"If we're going to be in here for three years, I

don't want to live in fear," said Kerri. "We need to do something about Officer Crowley."

"I'm glad you feel that way," said Mehgan, approval shining in her eyes as her gaze met Kerri's. "I'm confident that we could get the Blue Wolves to help us. I know they're picky about what they're willing to get involved with, but this is hardly a small matter, and really, it's something that concerns them too – and indeed, all of us."

"Exactly," said Kerri. "We can't sit back for three years, letting Crowley get away with this shit, all whilst each of us is wondering who his next victim might be."

"Leave it with me," Mehgan assured, determination resonating in her voice. "I'll talk to the Blue Wolves on my side of the wing."

A guard's announcement pierced through the ambience in the air, signalling the end of precious yard time. As Kerri and Mehgan reluctantly broke away from their intense conversation, in a silent vow of resolve, they walked back to their respective ends of the wing with fire in their eyes.

Chapter Fourteen

The clatter of trays and cutlery echoed through the canteen as Kerri sat next to Jayda in the far corner, their table cold and uncomfortable beneath their arms. On their trays was a sorry excuse for a meal – stale porridge that looked more like glue than food, and a pitiful cheese sandwich, the bread threatening to dissolve at the slightest touch.

Kerri couldn't care less about the food though. Her gaze was fixed on the Blue Wolves, huddled together at their own table on the opposite side of the canteen. She chewed her bottom lip, contemplating how Mehgan had managed to get so close to the Blue Wolves on her side of the wing. Sure, Mehgan had impressed the Blue Wolves in her refusal to take any shit from Stacey, but still Kerri lacked the confidence to form her own bonds with such a tough-looking group. What could she do, if anything, to befriend the Blue Wolves on her side of the wing and inspire their alliance?

"Earth to Kerri," Jayda said jokingly, her voice light and musical as she waved a hand in front of Kerri's face. "You're a million miles away."

"Oh," Kerri muttered, tearing her gaze away from the Blue Wolves. "Yeah, sorry. I've just got this gut feeling that something serious is about to go down."

Jayda raised an eyebrow, a playful grin tugging at the corners of her mouth.

"Are you sure it's not just the food that's making you feel bleak?"

Kerri shook her head, her long dark hair obscuring her sharp features for a moment.

"No, it's more than that," she said, her voice low and urgent, her eyes pleading with Jayda to understand. "It's not a witch's hunch or anything like that... it's more of a general sense of foreboding."

Jayda's expression softened, though her natural cheerfulness still shone through.

"I believe you, Kerri. But maybe we shouldn't dwell on things that haven't happened yet. They might not even come to pass. You'll drive yourself crazy."

"Just promise me that you'll stay alert," Kerri insisted.

"Ok," said Jayda.

It was clear to Kerri that Jayda didn't want to take on anything heavy.

"Anyway," said Kerri, accepting that Jayda didn't know the full story. "Get yourself over to the laundry. You hate being put on the tumble dryers."

"Yeah, that's true," Jayda replied. "They don't smell too good and the dust makes me cough."

With that, Jayda sauntered away from the table, her delicate wings shimmering with every step. She tossed her long hair over her shoulder and flashed a wink back at Kerri before disappearing around the corner towards the laundry room.

Left to herself, Kerri exhaled a deep breath and pushed her tray of uneaten food away. Her mind whirled, but she knew there was little she could do until her next catch-up with Mehgan. For now, she just needed to keep her head down and get on with things. With another heavy sigh, she left the table, emptied her tray of barely-touched food, and then made her way to the laundry.

***

Later that day, yard time finally arrived and the heavy doors creaked open. A surge of anticipation coursed through Kerri's veins as she stepped out into the open air, scanning the crowded area for any sign of her sister. This was her chance to find out if the Blue Wolves were in agreement about putting an end to Officer Crowley's brutal threats and violence against Sammi.

"Kerri!" Mehgan called out from across the yard.

"Hey!" Kerri shouted back as she wove her way through the throng of inmates, careful not to draw too much attention. "Mehgan, I've been dying to talk to you. What's happening?"

"We've got so much to tell you," Mehgan said as she nodded in the direction of the Blue

Wolves. "Come with me."

Kerri followed Mehgan's lead as they made their way towards the Blue Wolves from Mehgan's side of the wing. Lark, the muscular woman who Kerri had briefly spoken to before, stepped forward. With her intimidating stature, tattoos, and piercing gaze, she commanded attention.

"Listen up," she said, her voice gruff but certain. "We've come up with a plan to take down that piece of shit Crowley, but it's gonna require every single inmate working together."

"Ok," said Kerri. "What do we need to do?"

"When yard time next comes around, every witch in this hellhole needs to cast a sleep spell on every guard except Crowley," Lark instructed, her tone firm and authoritative. "Spread the word on your side of the wing. We'll handle the rest."

Kerri's stomach churned with dread at the responsibility being laid upon her shoulders. But then, she steeled herself, determined to focus on the bigger picture.

"I'll start by telling Jayda," she replied with a resolute nod. "She knows everyone; she'll help me spread the word."

"Good," Lark replied, her expression unyielding. "We can't afford any setbacks. If anyone tries to sabotage the plan, scare them off; tell them that they'll have me to answer to."

"Understood," Kerri murmured, feeling the importance of her task settle upon her.

Despite her nerves, Kerri felt certain that everyone was poised to do the right thing. They all shared the common goal of wanting to protect Sammi – and every other potential victim in the inmate population – from Officer Crowley's corruption.

Her passion fiercely ignited, Kerri was fired-up to rally the inmates on her side of the wing.

Chapter Fifteen

Over the next few days, Kerri worked tirelessly to spread the word about the plan. The tension in Grimlock Prison grew thick as anticipation built for the day of reckoning. Despite the high stakes, inmates from all corners of the paranormal spectrum rallied behind the cause, united in their desire to bring down Officer Crowley, and to protect one another.

One afternoon, when Kerri and Jayda were pushing a heavy laundry cart through the narrow corridors, Sammi appeared from around a corner. She looked exhausted, but determined, her eyes filled with a blend of gratitude and concern.

"Kerri," she called out, her voice hoarse but steady. "Can I talk to you for a moment?"

"Sure," Kerri replied.

Jayda gave Kerri an encouraging smile before heading off alone down the corridor with the cart.

Sammi led Kerri into her cell. There was something about the wolf shifter's mannerisms that seemed so honest, so stripped-back.

"Kerri, I just wanted to say thank you," Sammi began humbly, her eyes searching Kerri's face for understanding. "For everything you're doing to help me. To help all of us."

Kerri's heart clenched at the raw emotion in Sammi's voice.

"You're more than welcome," she said. "I can't stand by and let that bastard continue to terrorise you, or anyone else in this place."

"Still, it's dangerous," Sammi insisted, her voice cracking slightly. "You need to be careful, Kerri. There's no telling how Crowley might retaliate if he got word of the plan before it could be carried out."

"I know," Kerri whispered, her own fear clawing at her chest. "But it's worth the risk if it means keeping you safe."

In that moment, with their bodies mere inches

apart, time seemed to stand still. An electric current of longing and desire crackled in the air between them, beckoning them closer. Sammi's lips trembled as they progressed towards Kerri's, directed by an irresistible magnetic pull. Finally, with a tender yet passionate urgency, their mouths met in a kiss that cried volumes of their unspoken feelings for each other.

The rhythmic pounding of Kerri's pulse reverberated throughout her body as she pressed her lips against Sammi's. Every nerve ending seemed to ignite with the heat of their connection, a fire that had been smouldering between them for ages. She couldn't deny the pull she felt towards the strong and mysterious wolf shifter, the moment of vulnerability and closeness taking their dynamic to a whole new level – one that she had never dared to explore before. As their bodies moulded together, she could feel the raw power and primal energy coursing through her veins, stoking a yearning that refused to be tamed.

As they finally broke apart, both elated and flushed with passion, Kerri's gaze locked onto Sammi's eyes. Their depths shimmered like diamonds, reflecting the intensity of their shared moment.

"Please, Sammi. Stay strong for just a few more days. No matter what happens, no matter how hard Officer Crowley might try to pressure you and up the stakes, just know that the whole prison is behind you, and soon, that piece of shit will be made to pay for everything he's done to you."

Touched by Kerri's words, Sammi looked as though she was about to cry. Kerri wasn't going to let that happen though; she tenderly ran a finger along one of the bruises that Officer Crowley had so brutally left on Sammi's cheek. Although it was beginning to heal, its yellowish-green hue was undeniable, even in the dim light of the concrete cell.

"I won't let that bastard break you."

With that, they shared one last lingering glance before Kerri left the cell, her resolve strengthened by the knowledge that she was fighting not just for justice, but for someone she cared deeply about.

Chapter Sixteen

In its descent towards the horizon, the sun cast an orange glow across the prison yard. Despite the fair conditions, however, the tension in the air was beyond overwhelming.

Word of the plan had spread like wildfire through the prison. Every inmate on the wing, regardless of their affiliation or background, stood united. A shared sense of duty lingered, binding them together in a firm alliance.

Sweat trickled down Kerri's spine, her pulse quickening as the final moments before taking action unfolded and ticked away. With Mehgan by her side, the other witches huddled around her, their eyes meeting in silent understanding, each knowing the risks and stakes of what they were about to attempt.

"Fuck," Kerri muttered under her breath, trying to steady her nerves.

She couldn't help but think of Sammi and of everything the poor wolf shifter had suffered at the hands of Officer Crowley. She knew that beneath Sammi's tough exterior, was not only vulnerability, but a well of pain.

"Ok, everyone," Mehgan whispered, her voice barely audible amidst the tension-laden air. "Focus on your target. Remember to direct the spell at every guard but Crowley. We need him conscious."

Kerri nodded, swallowing hard. It was now or never. As the seconds drained away, she glanced over at the pack of Blue Wolves milling nervously nearby. They were counting on her and the other witches to pave the way for their retribution against Officer Crowley. Failure wasn't an option.

"Alright," Kerri said breathily, her heart pounding like a wild drum in her chest. "This is it."

She turned to her fellow witches, each one raising their hands in unison, their fingers tracing intricate patterns through the air.

"By the power of the ancients, we bind and

command thee," they chanted in hushed tones.

The energy between them thrummed as invisible threads began to weave themselves into a tangible force. A low hum permeated the atmosphere, growing louder and more insistent as the power of their collective magic swirled around them, and soon, the entire yard.

Focusing intently on the guards scattered throughout the yard, Kerri watched as one by one, they slumped to the ground, their eyes rolling back in their heads. As the witches' spell took hold, Kerri stood with a mixture of fear and triumph as she saw Officer Crowley still standing, his expression a blend of panic and confusion.

"Wh... what the fuck is happening?" he stammered, his gaze darting frantically around the yard in search of an explanation.

Kerri gritted her teeth as she watched the Blue Wolves spring into action. Two hulking members of the pack grabbed Crowley by the arms. They dragged him kicking and screaming into the centre of the yard. The other Blue Wolves then closed in, their menacing presence making it clear that they were ready to exact their revenge on the corrupt guard.

"Get your filthy hands off me!" Crowley shouted.

Despite his feeble attempt to exert authority, his voice trembled with fear. He knew he was cornered, and no amount of bluster could save him now.

A dark satisfaction coursed through Kerri's veins as she took in his panicked breaths, hitching in his throat as he kicked and screamed, desperately trying to escape the Blue Wolves' vice-like grip.

"Shut the hell up, Crowley," said Lark as she stepped forward with menacing authority. "You've got the whole damn prison against you. You're finished."

Good, Kerri thought, watching as the Blue Wolves prepared to deal with their deserving victim.

Every one of the Blue Wolves in the yard began to circle around Crowley, like predators closing in on their prey. Their sheer number, size and power loomed threateningly as a living embodiment of retribution. As they forced Officer Crowley down onto his knees, Kerri could almost feel the tremors of fear running through his body, echoing the terror he'd instilled in Sammi.

"Please," he begged, his voice shaking. "I didn't mean to..."

"Shut your fucking mouth," Lark said with a snarl as she took another step closer to Crowley, her piercing gaze locked onto his quivering form. "You piece of shit. How dare you ask an inmate to do your dirty work on the outside."

Kerri watched with bated breath. This was what they had been working towards. Before her was the culmination of whispered plans and true loyalties. The inmates were playing a dangerous game, but it was the only way to protect Sammi – and everyone else – from Crowley's corruption.

"Sammi's lying!" Crowley sputtered, his voice a thin wisp of diluted bravado. "She's just a typical inmate, making up stories for attention!"

Lark stepped in even closer to Crowley, her movements calculated and predatory. In a swift motion, her hand flew out and connected with a resounding smack, leaving a red mark blossoming on her target's cheek.

"I know Sammi isn't a member of the Blue Wolves, but fuck it, she's honourable," Lark said in a low growl, offended by the starkness of Crowley's audacity. "There's not a single prisoner in here willing to stand for your lies or your corruption any longer."

Every word Lark spoke felt like a hammer driving nails into the foundation of the inmates' newfound unity. Kerri could see tension in everyone, each prisoner coiled like a spring and ready to jump to an ally's defence if needed. She was certain that everyone was thinking the same thing: they refused to be victims.

Crowley flinched under Lark's unyielding gaze. He looked like a cornered animal, his eyes darting from one hostile face to another as he tried to find an escape.

"Please," he choked out, his voice barely audible. "Can we at least talk about this calmly?"

A cold, merciless smile etched itself onto Lark's

face as the Blue Wolves encircled Crowley.

"Don't take the piss," she uttered with a deep, guttural edge.

She delivered another shocking blow to the side of his face. It came swift and brutal, shaking every spectator to the core as they watched, adrenaline pounding through them like the rumble of thunder.

"Please," Officer Crowley whimpered. "I'm sorry!"

"You're just sorry that you got caught," another member of the Blue Wolves commented, her burly stature towering over the petrified prison guard.

Officer Crowley's eyes darted nervously as he flinched beneath the unyielding gaze of the Blue Wolves, their piercing stares like daggers penetrating his skin. His normally-healthy complexion was now a mottled pallor, with angry red flushes of humiliation. Every muscle in his body tensed as he tried to shrink away from their scrutiny, but there was no escaping the intense judgment.

In a frenzied blur of kicks and punches, the Blue Wolves unleashed a barrage of unrelenting blows upon Officer Crowley's body, the sound of flesh hitting flesh echoing throughout the yard. With calculated precision, they struck him with a ferocity that seemed to escalate each time. Lark, overseeing the scene with keen eyes, made sure that no violence went beyond the ultimate goal shared by all inmates: to assert dominance over their enemy.

"Enough!" she bellowed, her command slicing through the air like a whip.

The Blue Wolves abruptly halted their assault. They stepped back in unison, revealing the horrifying sight of Officer Crowley. As he lay broken and battered, crumpled on the ground, he trembled with terror. His face was a mess of blood and bruises, his features swollen and bent out of shape. A pool of crimson liquid seeped from his mouth and nose – mingling with the dirt beneath him, it painted a sickening picture.

Lark crouched down, and put her face right up close to Officer Crowley's, invading what little personal space he had left.

"If you ever breathe a word of this to anyone,

your life won't be worth living," she instructed, the venom in her words piercing the charged silence. "We don't want scum like you walking among us. You'd better leave Grimlock Prison – right now, and forever."

Crowley's eyes, swollen and bloodshot, met Lark's icy gaze. He nodded weakly, every ounce of defiance drained from his heavily pummelled body.

"Good," said Lark, rising to her full height. "Now get the fuck out of our sight."

Crowley swallowed hard, pain flashing across his features. He knew he had no choice but to accept the inmates' terms and leave Grimlock Prison behind forever. He struggled to his feet, wincing with every movement. His once-imposing figure now seemed small and pathetic, reduced to nothing more than a whimpering shell. Everyone watched as he limped away, leaving a trail of blood and shame in his wake.

The sight wasn't an easy one to take in. It left a bitter taste lingering in Kerri's mouth, but she couldn't deny the small flicker of relief that burned within her.

Justice, she thought, her heart still pounding. *At least for now.*

"Good riddance," said Mehgan, turning to address Kerri.

"I'm just glad it's over," said Kerri. "Let's just hope that we never have to do something like this again."

"I agree," said Mehgan, pulling her sister close.

And with that, everyone in the yard disappeared into the shadows, leaving the remnants of their brutal vengeance behind.

Epilogue

When the time came for the inmates to go inside at the end of yard time, with focus and precision, the witches wove an intricate spell. The delicate-yet-potent magic rippled through the prison, touching each sleeping guard with a veil of forgetfulness. In the aftermath of the spell, the guards stirred, awakening as if from a deep, dreamless sleep, completely unaware of the supernatural influence that had momentarily claimed their consciousness. As the inmates filed back into the prison, the success of the spell lingered like a secret shared among those who had orchestrated it. The yard, once a stage for rebellion, returned to its ordinary façade, concealing the inmates' intervention beneath the surface.

Weeks later, the corridors of Grimlock Prison bore witness to a profound metamorphosis. Officer Crowley's presence had become an elusive memory within its imposing walls, as if the very essence of his malevolence recoiled at the transformed atmosphere. The once-dreaded name had faded into whispers, and it seemed improbable that his authoritative shadow would ever darken the prison's threshold again.

The inmates, once wary of the notorious Blue Wolves, now regarded them with a newfound reverence. The gang's enigmatic aura had shifted from one of peril to that of protectors, their influence rippling through the prison's social fabric. The dynamics had altered, and the inmates found a sense of security in the unexpected alliance, turning a once-cautious division into an unspoken pact of safeguarding against external threats.

Amidst the evolving tapestry of change, Kerri and Sammi's connection continued to flourish. Their romance, an unyielding force, became a refuge against the unsettling realities of prison life. Sammi, no longer burdened by the threat of a blackmail-enforced parole, was free to serve the rest of her sentence with Kerri, finding solace in the companionship that continued to blossom within the sturdy confines.

For Kerri and Mehgan, their time in prison

would grow to be something better than an existence based on mere survival. Despite how magic-gone-wrong was the reason behind their three-year sentence, they found reassurance in the fact that they had been able to use their powers for something good, something that had succeeded to infuse a semblance of humanity into Grimlock Prison.

Through discreet spells and acts of compassion, Kerri and Mehgan would continue to alleviate the harshness of prison life, bringing small comforts and moments of respite to their fellow inmates. The frustration over their imprisonment had evolved into a driving force for positive change. They had, against all odds, turned a dark chapter in their lives into a narrative of resilience, hope, and unity.

9 781913 779238